Other books by Jeanne Willis and Adrian Reynolds

WHO'S IN THE LOO?

Winner of the Red House Children's Book Award
and the Sheffield Children's Book Award

For Anthony Waring. For lots of reasons. Love from J.W.

For Thomas, Célia, Max and Benjy – A.R.

First published in Great Britain in 2008 by Andersen Press Ltd.,
20 Vauxhall Bridge Road, London SW1V 2SA.
Published in Australia by Random House Australia Pty.,
Level 3, 100 Pacific Highway, North Sydney, NSW 2060.
Text copyright © Jeanne Willis, 2008. Illustration copyright © Adrian Reynolds, 2008
The rights of Jeanne Willis and Adrian Reynolds to be identified as the author and illustrator
of this work have been asserted by them in accordance with the Copyright, Designs and Patents Act, 1988.
All rights reserved. Colour separated in Switzerland by Photolitho AG, Zürich.
Printed and bound in Singapore by Tien Wah Press.

10   9   8   7   6   5   4   3   2   1

British Library Cataloguing in Publication Data available.

ISBN 978 1 84270 728 9

This book has been printed on acid-free paper

MINE'S BIGGER THAN YOURS!

Jeanne Willis   **Adrian Reynolds**

Andersen Press • London

Little Hairy Monster was sitting on a rock licking a lollipop, when along came . . .

SCARY MONSTER

"I'm bigger than you!" said Scary
Monster. "Give me your lollipop!"

But Little Hairy Monster wouldn't.
She got up and walked off.

Scary Monster walked after her.

"My feet are bigger than yours!" he said. "Give me your lollipop or I'll kick you!"

"No!" said Little Hairy Monster, and she stepped out of his way.

Scary Monster stepped after her.

"My tail is bigger than yours!" he said. "Give me your lollipop or I'll trip you!"

"No!" said Little Hairy Monster, and she skipped over his tail.

Scary Monster skipped after her.

"My legs are bigger than yours!" he said. "Give me your lollipop or I'll catch you!"

"No!" said Little Hairy Monster, and she ran as fast as her legs would carry her.

Scary Monster ran after her.
"My claws are bigger than yours!" he said. "Give
me your lollipop or I'll scratch you!"
"Hands off!" said Little Hairy Monster, and she
climbed up a tree.

"My paws are bigger than yours!" said Scary Monster. "Give me your lollipop or I'll shake you!"
"No!" said Little Hairy Monster.
Scary Monster shook her out of the tree. She ran off and hid inside a cave.

Scary Monster came sniffing all around. "My nose is bigger than your nose!" he said. "I can smell you! Give me your lollipop or I'll stink you out!" "Never!" thought Little Hairy Monster.

Scary Monster stood still and listened. "My ears
are bigger than yours!" he said. "I can hear you . . .
FOUND YOU! Give me your lollipop!"
"No!" roared Little Hairy Monster.

"My roar's bigger than yours!" laughed Scary Monster.
"Give me your lollipop or I'll deafen you . . .

rargggh hhh!"

"No, no, no!" said Little Hairy Monster,
and she put her hands over her ears.

Scary Monster opened his great big mouth. "My teeth are bigger than yours," he said. "Give me your lollipop or I'll bite you!"
"No!" said Little Hairy Monster. "Pick on someone your own size."

But Scary Monster was very hungry.
"My tummy is bigger than yours!" he said. "Give me your lollipop right now or I'll eat you!"

"I wouldn't do that if I were you,"
said Little Hairy Monster.
"Why not?" asked Scary Monster.
And she said, "Because . . .

. . . my mum is bigger than your mum!"